One Hot Day

Lynette Ruschak
Illustrated by May Rousseau

AN ARTISTS & WRITERS GUILD BOOK
Golden Books
Western Publishing Company, Inc.

One
hot
day
when
all
was
very
quiet,
the
ugliest
fish
swam
past
the
biggest
gorilla,

who
tried
to
grab
the
skinniest
snake
climbing
the
tallest
tree
in
the
jungle.

The
tallest
tree
was
home
to
the
fattest
bird,

who
flew
to
the
darkest
cave,
where
the
creepiest
bat

chased
the
prettiest
fluttering
butterfly

to
the
brightest
crimson
flower

that
hid
the
hairiest
caterpillar,

who
crawled
to
the
bluest
pond

and
scared
the
toothiest
crocodile
ever!

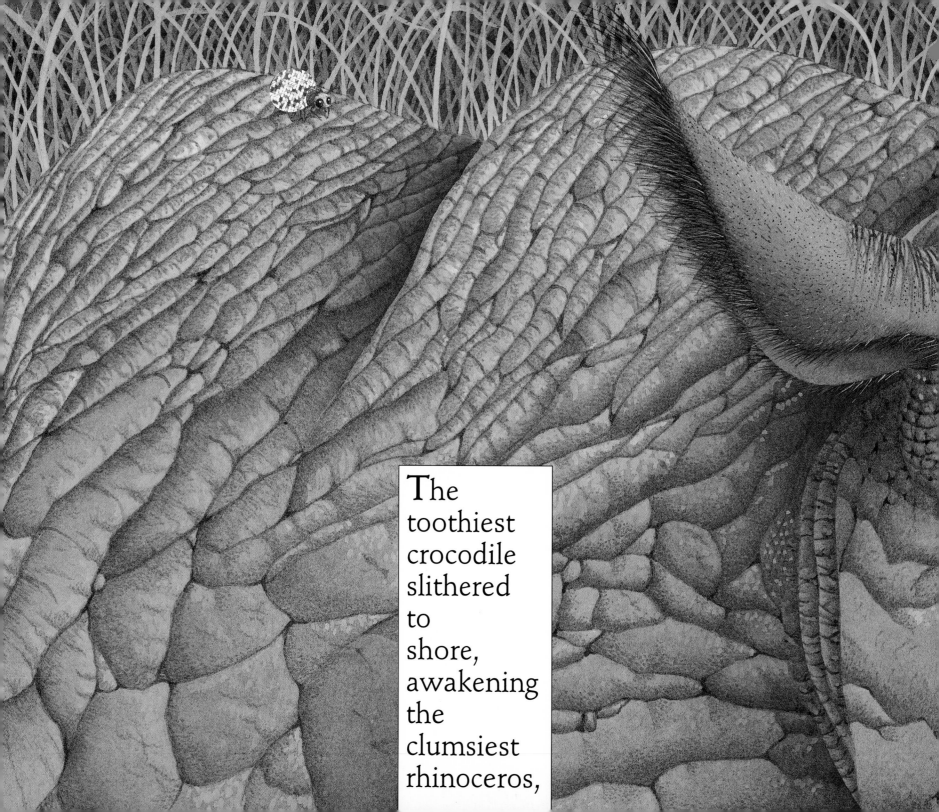

The
toothiest
crocodile
slithered
to
shore,
awakening
the
clumsiest
rhinoceros,

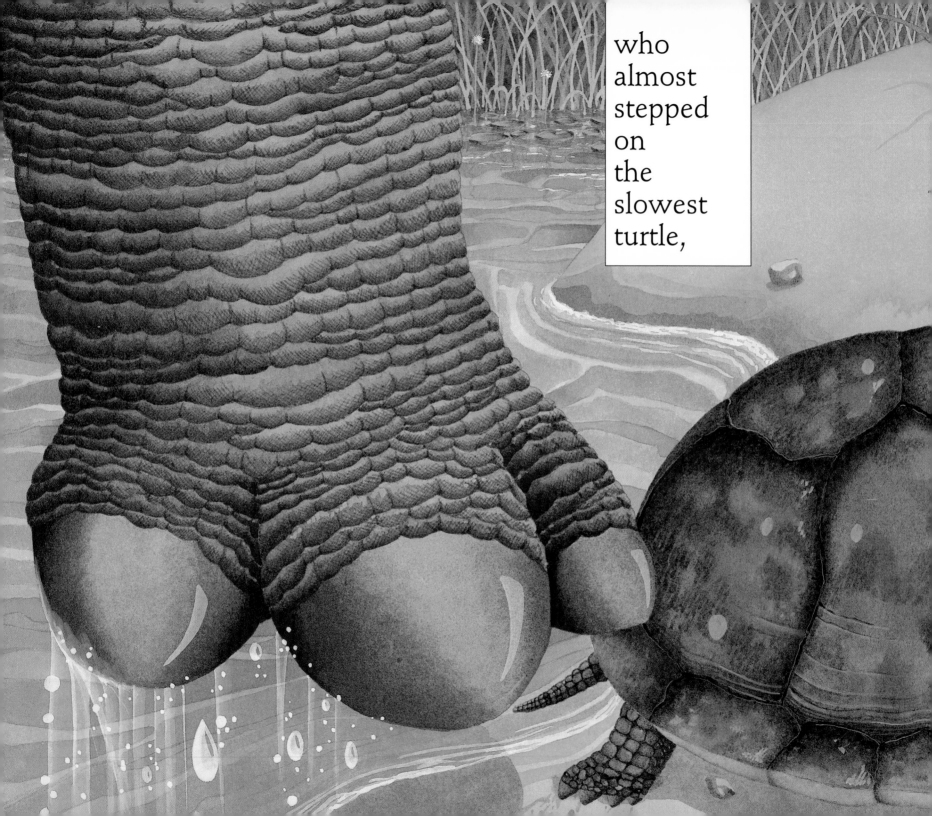

who
almost
stepped
on
the
slowest
turtle,

who
looked
at
the
prickliest
porcupine
and
laughed.

The prickliest porcupine fell in the muddiest puddle, almost crushing the shiniest bug.

The shiniest bug leaped for the largest lily pad,